Where Did Bunny Go?

A Bunny and Bird Story by

NANCY TAFURI

SCHOLASTIC PRESS   NEW YORK

Bunny and Bird lived
in an old apple tree.
They were best friends.

One morning, they saw
new snow all around.
"Do you want to play?" called Bunny.
"Yes!" said Bird.
She flew down to Bunny.

Bunny and Bird
jumped and hopped . . . .

and rolled together
in the new snow.

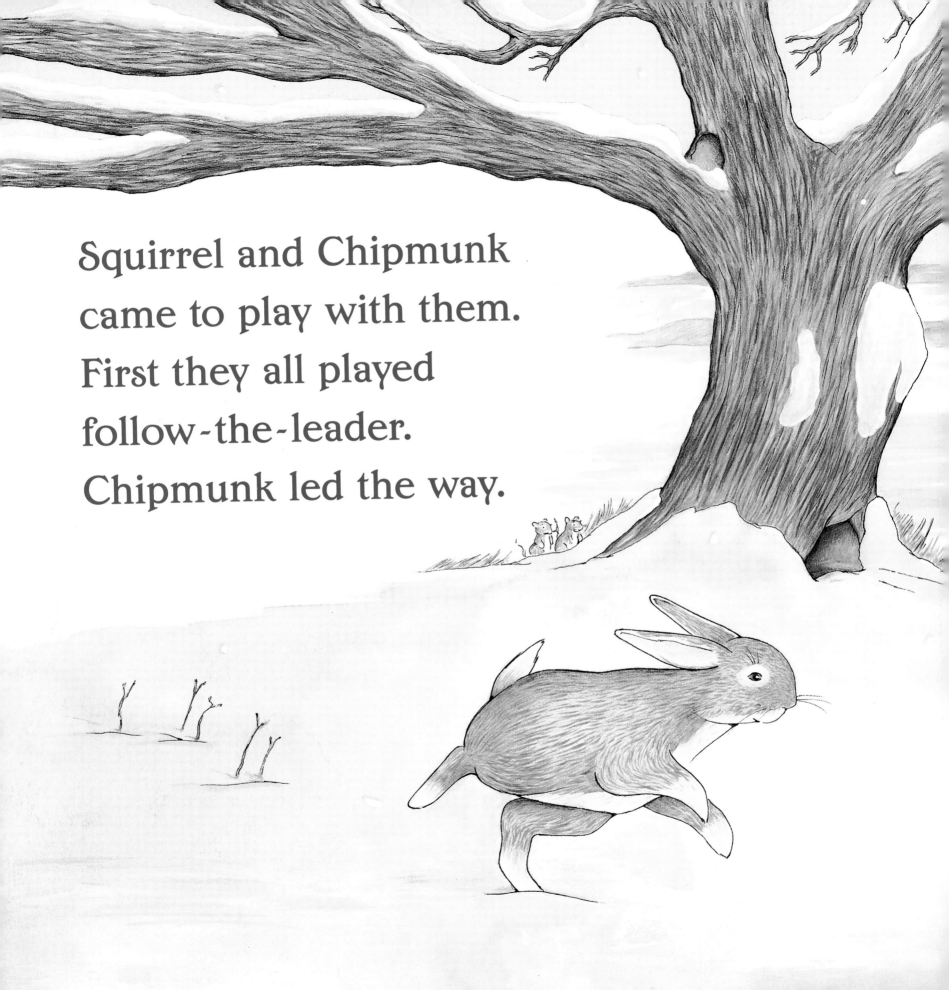

Squirrel and Chipmunk
came to play with them.
First they all played
follow-the-leader.
Chipmunk led the way.

Then they played hide-and-seek.
Bird covered her eyes.

Squirrel, Chipmunk, and Bunny
looked for good places
to hide.

Chipmunk ran
to the woods.

Squirrel ran
to the meadow.

Bunny hopped to the pond to hide.

Bird looked all around.

She found Squirrel
in a hollow of a tree trunk.

She found Chipmunk
under a bush.

Then Bird looked for Bunny.
She could not find him anywhere.
"Come out, Bunny!" called Bird.
Bunny did not come out.

"Where did Bunny go?"
asked Bird.

"We will help you look for him," said Chipmunk. "We will find Bunny together," said Squirrel.

They looked all around the meadow.
Bunny was not there.

"Maybe Bunny ran away,"
said Chipmunk.

"No," said Bird.
"Bunny is our friend.
He would not run away."

They looked all around the woods.
Bunny was not there.

"Maybe Bunny is lost,"
said Squirrel.

"I hope not," said Bird.
"We must keep looking."

They looked all around the pond.
They could not find Bunny anywhere.

Now Bird felt sad.

"Maybe Chipmunk is right,"
said Bird.

"Bunny ran away.
He does not want to play
with us anymore."

Then Bunny jumped out
of his hiding place.
"Here I am, Bird!" he called.

Bunny hopped over to Bird.
"I would never run away,"
said Bunny.
"I am your friend."

Then Bird felt happy again.
She flew into the air.
"I am glad you are
my friend," said Bird.
"I am glad you are
my <u>best</u> friend," said Bunny.

Then Bunny and Bird
and Chipmunk and Squirrel

played tag together
around the old apple tree.

To Cristina

LIBRARY OF CONGRESS CATALOGING-IN-PUBLICATION DATA

Tafuri, Nancy. Where did Bunny go?: a bunny and bird story / by Nancy Tafuri. – 1st ed.   p. cm.

Summary: Bird cannot find Bunny during a game of hide-and-seek

and worries that Bunny has run away.

ISBN 0-439-16959-3

[1. Rabbits – Fiction. 2. Birds – Fiction. 3. Hide-and-seek – Fiction.

4. Best friends – Fiction. 5. Friendship – Fiction.] I. Title.

PZ7.T117 Wge 2001   [E]—dc21 00-045007

10 9 8 7 6 5 4 3 2 1   01 02 03 04 05

Printed in Mexico 49

First edition, October 2001

The illustrations were painted in watercolors and inks.

The text was set in 32-point Edwardian Medium.

Design by Nancy Tafuri and David Saylor